Look out for all *The Fairy House* books:

FAIRY FRIENDS
FAIRY FOR A DAY
FAIRIES TO THE RESCUE
FAIRY RIDING SCHOOL
FAIRY SLEEPOVER
FAIRY JEWELS

Other books by Kelly McKain

Mermaid Rock:
PIRATE TROUBLE
SPOOKY SHIPWRECK
TREASURE HUNT
WHALE RESCUE

Make sure you visit www.thefairyhouse.co.uk
for competitions, prizes and lots more fairy fun!

The Fairy House

Fairy Jewels

Welcome to the Fairy House –
a whole new magical world...

The Fairy House
Fairy Jewels

Kelly McKain

Illustrated by Nicola Slater

■SCHOLASTIC

First published in the UK in 2008 by Scholastic Children's Books
An imprint of Scholastic Ltd
Euston House, 24 Eversholt Street
London, NW1 1DB, UK
Registered office: Westfield Road, Southam, Warwickshire, CV47 0RA
SCHOLASTIC and associated logos are trademarks and or registered trademarks
of Scholastic Inc.

Text copyright © Kelly McKain, 2008
Illustration copyright © Nicola Slater, 2008

The right of Kelly McKain and Nicola Slater to be identified as the author and
illustrator of this work has been asserted by them.

Cover illustration © Nicola Slater, 2008

ISBN 978 1 407 10361 7

A CIP catalogue record for this book
is available from the British Library

Printed and bound by Imago
Papers used by Scholastic Children's Books are made from
wood grown in sustainable forests.

1 3 5 7 9 10 8 6 4 2

This is a work of fiction. Names, characters, places, incidents and dialogue are
products of the author's imagination or are used fictitiously. Any resemblance to
actual people, living or dead, events or locales is entirely coincidental.

www.kellymckain.co.uk
www.scholastic.co.uk/zone

For the lovely Miss Poppy Belderbos xx

Chapter 1

Katie stepped out into the garden and whirled round and round on the lawn, arms outstretched. It was the first day of the summer holidays – at last! She was so excited. No more sitting in a stuffy classroom filled with noise and chatter. No more bells and books and lonely playtimes. No more Tiffany Towner being mean to her. With no more school, she could spend all day every day in the

almost-meadow with her new friends. Her new *fairy* friends. It was going to be the best summer ever! And it was starting right now!

Katie patted her pocket and grinned to herself. She had something very special tucked inside and she couldn't wait to show it to the fairies. At the bottom of her garden, she wriggled under the wire fence, which was now heavy with white-flowered bindweed, and dashed across the almost-meadow. Wild grasses, vibrant with foxgloves and dandelions, brushed her legs and all around her the air was filled with birds and bees and butterflies.

When Katie reached the Magic Oak tree, she couldn't see the fairies anywhere. That was strange. They were usually playing flying tag in

its canopy of lush green leaves or doing handstands on its gnarled roots. She stepped carefully over Daisy's handkerchief hammock and crouched down by the Fairy House.

The Fairy House used to be Katie's dolls' house, but when she'd accidentally left it outside under the oak tree one night, Snowdrop, Bluebell, Daisy and Rosehip had moved in. Katie had been firm friends with the four fairies ever since, and she'd given them the house for their very own. Now, she put her little finger on the enchanted doorknob and whispered the magic words "I believe in fairies, I believe in fairies, I believe in fairies." Then she giggled as the top of her head tingled and, with a great whooshing sound in her ears, she shrank down, down, down to

fairy size. Then, her heart leaping with excitement about the special surprise in her pocket, she stepped into the Fairy House.

"Hi, I'm here!" she cried, peering round the doorway into the living room.

But there was no one on the sofa, with its rose-petal throw, and no one lounging on the woven-grass rug. The kitchen, with its cheery pink chequered tablecloth and pressed flowers taped to the cupboards, was empty too.

"Bluebell? Daisy?" called Katie, but there was no reply.

She hurried up the stairs and found her friends sitting silently on Bluebell's bed, heads bowed over a piece of paper. Daisy was nervously chewing the end of one of her plaits and Rosehip was jiggling her legs

anxiously. Snowdrop's thick black hair had fallen forward across her face as she frowned down at the paper. Even boisterous Bluebell was silent.

"What's up?" Katie asked, making them all jump.

"Oh, hello!" said Rosehip. "We didn't even hear you come in. We were all too busy *thinking*!"

Katie kicked off her shoes and climbed on to the bed as well. As soon as she saw what the fairies were

staring at, she knew exactly why they looked so serious. It was the scroll from the Fairy Queen, and Katie had seen it many times before. It read:

Fairy Task No. 45826

By Royal Command of the Fairy Queen

Terrible news has reached Fairyland. As you know, the Magic Oak is the gateway between Fairyland and the human world. The sparkling whirlwind can only drop fairies off here. Humans plan to knock down our special tree and build a house on the land. If this happens, fairies will no longer be able to come and help people and the environment. You must stop them from doing this terrible thing and make sure that the tree is protected for the future. Only then will you be allowed back into Fairyland.

By order of Her Eternal Majesty
The Fairy Queen

P.S. You will need one each of the twelve birthstones to work the magic that will save the tree - but hurry, there's not much time!

Of course, Katie had already promised to help the fairies in their task. "We're doing brilliantly. We've already collected five birthstones," she reminded them.

"But that means we've still got seven to find," said Daisy. "Erm, doesn't it?"

Katie nodded. Maths was not the fairies' strong point. "Yes, we still need amethyst, aquamarine, diamond, emerald, pearl, ruby and turquoise," she said, counting them off on her fingers as she spoke.

"And we just can't work out how to get even *one* of them," wailed Snowdrop. "My brain hurts from thinking so hard and we still haven't had any good ideas."

Katie couldn't help smiling then.

"Katie! This is serious!" cried Bluebell. "What if Max Towner's

getting ready to knock the Magic Oak down *right now*? We don't have the power to stop him!"

Max Towner was the developer behind the plans to demolish the tree and build a luxury villa in its place. He was also the father of the revolting Tiffany, the girl who made Katie's life a misery at school.

But Katie was still smiling. She took the special something out of her pocket. It had shrunk down to fairy size along with her. The fairies frowned at it, confused.

"I don't see how showing us a chocolate bar wrapper will help and I don't—" Bluebell began, but Katie just smiled, smoothed it out and began to read.

"Join in the fabulous Chocolate Time treasure hunt and win a ruby!"

She paused, eyes twinkling. As

she continued, the fairies squashed in close to her, to see for themselves.

"'We've buried six little treasure chests, each containing a *real* ruby, at different locations around the country. Join us at your nearest treasure hunt on Saturday 30th July between twelve noon and three p.m. For every two chocolate bar wrappers sent in you will receive one clue as to the whereabouts of your nearest buried treasure. Good luck!'"

"Katie, that's brilliant!" cried Rosehip, hugging her.

"You're such a great friend!" added Daisy, joining in the hug and pulling Snowdrop in too.

Bluebell jumped up and down with excitement, making the bed shake so much that they nearly tumbled off. "We'll win the treasure hunt and get the ruby!" she sang, over and over again.

Katie squinted at the small print on the wrapper. "It says here that there are six clues you can send for, so we need to get twelve wrappers to have the best chance of winning," she told them.

"Is that a lot?" asked Snowdrop.

Katie nodded. "Yes, especially as the treasure hunt is on Saturday. We really need to send the wrappers off today to be sure of getting the clues back in time."

Snowdrop looked downcast at this, but Bluebell was as enthusiastic as ever. She leapt off the bed,

clapped her hands and cried, "In that case, we'd better get cracking!"

Chapter 2

Of course, Mum wouldn't give Katie enough money to buy eleven chocolate bars, even just to enter the treasure hunt. But she did say that she could have her pocket money early if she did her jobs (which were dusting the living room and tidying all the coats and shoes in the hall). That would get them two more bars, which was a start.

Katie got straight to work and Mum was amazed when she

finished in only a few minutes – but then, Mum didn't know she had four fairy helpers!

Seeing how keen Katie was to get to the shop, Mum offered to walk up to the village with her right away. On the way, the four fairies flew high above them, turning excited cartwheels and loop the loops in the air.

When they reached the centre of the village, Mum bumped into a friend and they decided to go for a cup of tea together. She gave Katie a kiss and told her to walk down to the café when she was ready. Full of excitement, Katie (and the fairies) went into the newsagent's.

The fairies were amazed to see so many shiny chocolate wrappers and brightly coloured jars of sweets. In fact, they completely forgot that

they were there to buy Chocolate Time bars and wanted to try *everything*!

Katie bought the chocolate bars and they all sat on the bench outside and ate them.

"That's three wrappers," she said, when the last bite was gone. "But how are we going to get *twelve*?"

"Is twelve more than three, then?" asked Snowdrop.

"Yes, a *lot* more," said Katie.

The fairies' little shoulders drooped and they looked very downcast. Katie tried not to show it but she felt as glum as they did.

Just then a gust of wind blew up and sent something scuttling along beside the bench. Something shiny, with *Chocolate Time* written on it.

"Quick! Follow that wrapper!" shouted Bluebell.

The fairies zoomed after it, with Katie sprinting along behind them. Finally the wrapper got stuck in a hedge and Bluebell and Rosehip raced to grab it, forgot to put the brakes on and got tangled in the hedge too! In the end it was Daisy who plucked out the wrapper and held it up proudly.

"Well done!" puffed Katie as she caught up with them, thoroughly

out of breath. "That makes four."

"But where on earth are we going to get the rest?" asked Snowdrop.

"I know we happen to need this wrapper, but people really shouldn't drop litter," said Bluebell huffily. "It should have been put in the bin!"

They all looked at her, grins

spreading across their faces.

"Bluebell, that's it!" Daisy exclaimed.

"What's it?" asked Bluebell, completely confused.

"The bin!" they all cried, and zoomed off again.

"Wait for me!" called Bluebell, taking off too.

Soon they were back outside the newsagent's, staring at the bin. Katie wriggled her hand through the hole in the centre but she couldn't reach anything.

"Oh dear, I suppose we'll just have to think of another way to get more wrappers..." she said. "Unless..." She looked at the fairies hopefully.

Rosehip tossed her flame-red hair and gave a snort of disgust. "*Fairies* don't go rummaging in bins!" she said haughtily.

"Our dresses will get all dirty," added Snowdrop with a shudder.

"And what about our hair?" squealed Daisy. "We might get *yucky bits* in it!"

"Girls," said Bluebell firmly, "I don't want to go into a bin either. But we need that ruby. And to have a chance of winning it we *must* get more wrappers – and there might be some in that bin!"

"OK, I'll go in if you do," said Rosehip nervously.

Bluebell smiled, and Katie said, "Well done, Rosehip and you, Bluebell. You're both very brave."

Daisy and Snowdrop didn't want to be left out of being brave, so they joined the others on the edge of the bin, holding their noses, their eyes screwed up.

"One, two, three, dive!" called

Bluebell, and they all jumped into the pile of rubbish below.

Katie peered in, watching the rubbish bob around.

There were squeals of "Urgh!" and "Yuck!", then suddenly a fairy hand appeared and threw a Chocolate Time wrapper up to Katie.

"Thanks!" she called, grabbing it

out of the air.

After a while the fairies bobbed back up, panting and making disgusted faces. Snowdrop handed one more wrapper to Katie.

"That's all there is," panted Daisy.

Rosehip shuddered. "All that disgustingness for only two wrappers! How on earth are we going to get the rest?"

A voice behind Katie demanded, "What *are* you doing?"

The fairies all ducked down under the rubbish. They recognized that voice and they didn't like it. Not one bit.

"Hello, Tiffany," said Katie.

Before Katie could shove them into her pocket, Tiffany caught sight of the wrappers.

"You might get *your* Chocolate Time bars out of the bin," she

sneered, "but I'm going to the shop," and with that she strode off into the newsagent's.

As the fairies climbed out of the bin, Katie saw that they had made disguises from the rubbish, so that Tiffany didn't spot them. "Good thinking, girls!" she said, as they heaved themselves up on to the rim of the bin.

When Tiffany reappeared and sat on the bench guzzling Chocolate Time bars, Bluebell peered out from beneath her lolly-wrapper disguise.

"We really need

more wrappers," she whispered. "Katie, maybe you could. . ."

Katie grimaced. They still needed six wrappers and she had no other ideas about where they were going to get them from. She knew Bluebell was right.

"OK, wish me luck," she said, and sloped over to the bench.

Tiffany ignored Katie and continued to guzzle the chocolate without offering her so much as a single piece.

"Why were you talking to a bin?" she asked at last, with her mouth full. "You're even more of a weird girl than I thought."

Katie pulled on a smile – much as she disliked Tiffany, she knew she had to be nice to her. "That chocolate

looks yummy," she said brightly.

"I'm not giving you any, you know," came the snooty reply.

"Oh, I don't mind," said Katie carefully, trying not to look bothered. "I could, maybe, take the wrappers, though, to put in the bin. It would save you the effort."

Tiffany smoothed out the wrappers from the three bars she'd

just polished off and held them out to Katie. But when she went to take them, Tiffany snatched her hand away.

"I know you're up to something," she said, smirking unkindly. "Hmm, what can it be?" She turned the wrappers over and over, then suddenly cried, "Aha! A treasure hunt!"

Katie sighed. She hadn't wanted to tell Tiffany about it but now she had no choice. When she'd finished explaining about the clues and the ruby and how she only had half of the wrappers she needed, Tiffany looked thoughtful.

"I'll give you the other six wrappers," she said slowly, "*if* you let me come along with you on Saturday."

Katie bit her lip. The last thing

she wanted was for Tiffany to be involved. But they really needed those wrappers right now or they wouldn't get the clues in time. She took a deep breath and muttered, "OK."

"Good," said Tiffany. "But *I'll* find the ruby, and when I do I don't want *you* sharing my prize. Finders keepers, all right?"

Katie agreed – anything to get those wrappers.

Tiffany finished scoffing her chocolate bars, handed the six wrappers to Katie and then stalked off without another word.

As the fairies threw off their disguises and flew over, Katie leaned back against the bench and sighed. "I'm sorry she has to come," she told them.

"Me too! She *kidnapped* me,

remember?" cried Daisy. "*And* I had to pretend to be a doll in case she found out about us fairies *and* she nearly snapped my wing off. She's horrible and mean and—"

But Bluebell interrupted her. "We've got the wrappers – that's all that matters," she said firmly, and, much as Tiffany frightened her, Daisy had to agree.

Katie went into the café and got a stamp from Mum, wrote her name and address on a napkin, then put everything into an envelope the café owner had given her. As she popped it into the postbox, the fairies spun and danced around her head in celebration.

Katie sniffed the air and wrinkled up her nose. "Poo! You lot really need a bath!" she cried, giggling.

"Fairies don't usually have baths!" said Daisy.

"Well, that's because fairies don't usually go rummaging around in bins!" cried Rosehip, and they all burst out laughing.

Katie felt her stomach flip with excitement. They had the wrappers. They'd sent off for all six clues. Now they just had to win the treasure hunt and the ruby would be theirs!

Chapter 3

Katie spent the rest of the day, and the day after that, playing with the fairies in the almost-meadow, visiting Auntie Jane and helping Mum water and weed the garden. But all the time, in the back of her mind, she was counting the hours until Friday morning's post, when the clues would arrive.

On Friday Katie was up bright and early, and as soon as she heard the postman crunching up the

gravel drive, she dashed downstairs. An envelope addressed to her landed on the mat. She scooped it up and ran through the house, grabbing Mum's *Guide to the West Country* on the way. "I'm going to the almost-meadow to work out the clues," she called out to Mum as she pushed back the bindweed and slipped under the wire fence.

When Katie arrived at the Magic Oak tree the fairies were sitting outside it on the pink chequered tablecloth, eager to help solve the clues. Katie kept hold of the *Guide to the West Country* as she touched the doorknob and chanted the magic words, so that when she shrank to fairy size it turned small too. She dashed over to her friends and plopped herself down. Then, after giving them all a big hello hug, she

spread out the clues. They squinted down at them, shading their eyes from the bright sunshine.

Once upon a time there was

a drink of water. But he knew if he did

a hot day, and wished he could have

he wouldn't be able to keep an eye on his treasure."

a green giant who lived on a hill.
He got very thirsty, for it was

Katie and the fairies frowned down at the slips of paper. It wasn't as easy as they had imagined.

"These don't make any sense," cried Bluebell. "It's hopeless! We'll never win the ruby!"

Katie picked up one of the clues. "Maybe it's not six different clues but six parts of one clue," she said thoughtfully. "'Once upon a time' could be the beginning. Because it's what you say to start off a fairy story."

"Once upon a time there was *what*, though?" asked Daisy, puzzled.

"A drink of water?" suggested Rosehip.

Bluebell snorted. "No one would write a fairy story about a drink of water, would they?" she teased. "That would be a bit boring!"

Rosehip folded her arms. "OK, *you* try then, if you're so clever," she said sulkily.

Bluebell squinted hard at the clues and confidently said, "Once upon a time there was a hot day."

Rosehip smiled smugly. "That doesn't sound right. See, it's harder than it looks!" And with that the two feistiest fairies started arguing about whose idea was better.

"Once upon a time there was a green giant who lived on a hill," said Snowdrop shyly, through the shouting.

"That's it!" cried Katie, and even Bluebell and Rosehip stopped arguing then and gave their shy little friend a big cheer.

"Well done, Snowdrop," said Daisy, beaming. "And that helps us work out what comes next, because

32

it says the giant got very thirsty, so we know it was a hot day!"

The fairies squealed with excitement as Katie placed that clue next to the first one.

Working together, they'd soon put the story into the right order, so that it went:

Once upon a time there was

a green giant who lived on a hill. He got very thirsty, for it was

a hot day, and wished he could have

a drink of water. But he knew if he did

he wouldn't be able to keep an eye on his treasure.

"So, which giant do you think they're talking about?" Katie asked them.

"There's a giant in 'Jack and the Beanstalk', maybe it's him," Bluebell suggested.

"But he didn't live on a hill, he lived up a beanstalk," Rosehip pointed out. "Or the story would have been called 'Jack and the Hill'."

Bluebell stuck her tongue out at Rosehip, who pulled a rude face back at her.

"Maybe we should look in my book," Katie said, "although it probably won't have any fairy-tale giants in it." She thumbed through to the index, looked up giants and was amazed to see that there *was* one!

She found the right page, then turned the book around for the fairies to see. The title said "The Cerne Abbas Giant" and there was a picture of a giant carved into the hillside, his white chalk outline clear and sharp against the dark green grass.

"*He's* a green giant!" Daisy exclaimed.

"He must be the one!" squealed Snowdrop, clapping her delicate hands in delight.

Katie turned to the fold-out map at the front of the book and found the village of Cerne Abbas. "It's not too far from here either," she told them.

They'd found the right giant, she was sure of it. But they still couldn't work out what the water that the giant wanted to drink might be. Eventually they had to give up.

Katie got to her feet and stretched her arms above her head. "We'll just have to go to the giant tomorrow and hope that the rest makes sense," she told her friends.

"In the meantime we could practise our treasure hunting," Bluebell suggested.

36

They all agreed that that was a very good idea. So, for the rest of the  morning they played treasure hunts in the almost-meadow, taking turns to bury things and making up clues so that the others could find them. It was so much fun! When they all sat down for a rest, Bluebell brought out some scrap material and Snowdrop's sewing kit from one of the kitchen cupboards and started making something.

Rosehip stood over her, frowning, her hands on her hips. "And what on earth is *that*?" she asked.

"You'll see," said Bluebell, smiling a mysterious smile. Then she bent her head back over her sewing and stuck out her tongue in concentration.

About half an hour later, Bluebell called out, "Finished!" and proudly held up her creation for them to see.

Katie and the fairies all stared at it, puzzled.

"It's very *nice*," said kind little Daisy, "but, erm, what is it exactly?"

"It's a treasure-hunting jacket, of course!" cried Bluebell. "It's got pockets to keep wild strawberry sherbet and bottles of water in, in case it's a very long treasure hunt and I get thirsty or I need something sweet to keep me going!"

"Oh, I see," said Katie.

The treasure-hunting jacket was,

well, *wonky* to say the least.

Daisy and Snowdrop smiled at Bluebell, but Rosehip burst into giggles and cried, "Oh, Bluebell, that thing looks awful! Your stitching's atrocious!"

Bluebell stamped her foot crossly. "Well, when you want a drink and some delicious sherbet tomorrow, don't come flying to me!" she said haughtily.

She waggled her tongue at Rosehip, put the jacket on, tied it up at the front with wild grass stems and refused to take it off for the rest of the morning.

After lunch, Mum took Katie for a

lovely walk in the fields and then they watched a film and read a story together. And all the time, Katie was daydreaming about the fun and excitement (and who knew, maybe even the ruby!) that the following day would bring.

Chapter 4

Katie paced anxiously up and down the hall on Saturday lunchtime – Tiffany was almost half an hour late. The treasure hunt had already begun and it was due to end at three p.m. Katie was worried they wouldn't make it in time – after all, they had to get to the giant and then finish working out the rest of the clue before they could even find the right place!

Mum wasn't in the best of moods

either, not after Katie had explained that Tiffany was coming with them. Tiffany had invited herself round once before (and then forced Katie to do her homework for her!) On that occasion, she'd been so horrible and rude that Mum was quite happy never to set eyes on her again. Only the fairies were cheerful, doing gymnastics on the washing line in the back garden. Bluebell was still wearing her treasure-hunting jacket, despite Rosehip's comments, and had filled one of the pockets with wild strawberry sherbet.

At long last the bell rang and Katie sprang to the door. Tiffany was standing on the doorstep in designer jeans and a red top that looked brand new.

"I like your dress, Katie," she

said, with a mean look on her face that showed she didn't really like it at all.

"Thank you," said Katie. She didn't want to start an argument. If she and Tiffany fell out, Mum might refuse to take them on the treasure hunt.

The fairies flew through the living-room window just as Mum was closing it and zoomed along the wall in the hallway, keeping out of sight. Katie opened her bag and they all jumped in. She had made them double promise on fairies' honour that they'd stay out of Tiffany's sight. If *she* got hold of them, who knew what she'd do?

Katie had to try really hard not to fall out with Tiffany on the way to Cerne Abbas, because all she did was moan and make snide

comments. First of all, she couldn't believe she had to ride in the back seat. *Her* dad always let her sit up front, she said. And she found it ridiculous that you had to wind the windows down by hand instead of pressing a button. *Her* car had electric ones. And however did they manage without a CD player? *Her* mum insisted on the latest model.

"Well, it's a pity *your* mum couldn't take us, then," said Katie, rolling her eyes.

"Oh, she's far too busy to be bothered with a stupid treasure hunt," Tiffany snapped. "She always spends Saturdays at the beauty salon."

Katie really wanted to say, "Well, if the treasure hunt is so stupid why are you coming, then?" but she stopped herself. Instead she just

sighed and looked out of the window. She put her bag up to the sill so that the fairies could look out too and get some fresh air.

When they finally arrived in Cerne Abbas it was nearly half past one and Katie was feeling anxious about the time. They got out of the car and stood staring up at the giant on the hill. When they were sure that Tiffany wasn't looking, the fairies poked their heads out of Katie's bag and stared too. There were a few people milling around in the car park, taking photos of the giant, but there was no treasure hunt.

"Well, there's no one here. You obviously got the wrong place," Tiffany accused.

Katie pretended not to hear her. She'd spotted an information board next to the giant's field, so she grabbed Mum's hand and hurried over to it, with Tiffany following sulkily behind. It was mainly about how old the giant was and everything, but there was a bit about the village of Cerne Abbas as well, and a map.

"Look, Mum," cried Katie. "There's a well in the village. That's where the giant could get a drink of water!"

"Read out the clue again, darling," said Mum thoughtfully.

"'Once upon a time there was a green giant who lived on a hill. He got very thirsty, for it was a hot day,

and wished he could have a drink of water. But he knew if he did he wouldn't be able to keep an eye on his treasure.'"

"I think the treasure is hidden at the well," Tiffany suddenly announced.

"I don't," said Katie quietly, checking the clue again, then the map.

Tiffany sighed and rolled her eyes, but Mum nodded encouragingly, so Katie went on.

"The clue says the giant can't go to the well because he needs to keep an eye on his treasure. We can see from this map that the well is down *behind* the hill. So what can he see from here that he couldn't see from the well?"

They all turned to see where the giant was looking. His round green

eyes gazed out on to a wooded hill. A flag was waving in the field just below it.

"Oh, I see! Over there!" cried Mum. "He couldn't see that flag from the well because his hill would be in the way. Well done, my clever girl!"

As she and Katie hugged each other, Tiffany fiddled with the Velcro on her trainer, furious that Katie had come up with the answer.

The fairies did a happy dance in

the air and then plopped, one by one, into Katie's bag.

When they were all back in the car, Mum set off up a lane, towards the flag.

"It's here!" Katie cried, as she spotted a turning with another flag beside it.

They parked and got out of the car, then followed the flags down the track to the field beyond.

Just then a cheery-looking man strode up to greet them. "Welcome to the treasure hunt! I'm Billy," he said. "You get one marker per set of clues and you must plant it in the spot where you think the treasure is."

Grinning, Katie handed over the clues and took the white marker from Billy. But then her face fell as she looked around. "You mean, we have to guess where the treasure is

in all of this?" she gasped.

The fields and woodland suddenly seemed to stretch for miles.

Billy smiled. "Well, you do get a bit of help. Here's the final clue."

He held a piece of card out to Katie but Tiffany snatched it away.

"Tiffany!" said Mum sharply, but she refused to give it back.

"*And* I want my own marker," she demanded.

Katie screwed up her fists, feeling that if she had to spend one more second with this revolting girl, she was going to scream, or cry, or both.

Tiffany made such a fuss that in the end Billy gave her a marker. Luckily he winked at Katie and handed her another copy of the final clue.

"Thank you," she said, relieved.

"Right, I'm off to hunt for the treasure," Tiffany announced, marching off across the field. "I'm going to win and you're going to lose, weird girl!" she shouted back over her shoulder.

Katie just sighed.

"I do apologize," Mum said to Billy. "She's not my daughter."

As Billy strolled away, Katie read the final clue to Mum extra loudly to make sure that the fairies could hear too. "What you seek is in the wrong place at the wrong time, but you'll need to be in the right place at the right time to find it."

Katie thought and thought, but she didn't understand what the clue meant. And neither did Mum.

Seeing the confusion on Katie's face, Mum squeezed her hand.

"As there's not much time, let's

split up and have a wander around, to see if we can find anything unusual that might fit the clue," she suggested. "Something that's in the wrong place. I'll have a look in the lane and up at the woods if you scout around the field."

Katie agreed and as soon as she set off, the fairies came zooming out of her bag, keen to help.

Together they set out across the field, looking for anything that might be in the wrong place at the wrong time.

After a while they spotted an old-fashioned train carriage with peeling blue paint by the fence and hurried over to it. There were lots and lots of white markers planted all the way around it.

"A train carriage is certainly out of place in a field, isn't it?" she muttered.

She was just about to stick the marker into the ground with the others when Bluebell shouted, "Stop!"

They all stared at her.

"There's nothing to do with the wrong *time* here," she reasoned. "Why don't we keep looking for as long as we can and then, when it

gets near the end, we can decide
where to put the marker?"

"Good idea, Bluebell," said Katie.

They were just about to set off
again when Snowdrop spotted
Tiffany coming towards them.

"Quick, hide!" she hissed,
and they all ducked
out of sight.

On seeing the
railway carriage,
Tiffany looked
delighted, sure
she'd found the
right place.
While she was
crouching down,
deciding where to
plant her marker, Katie and the
fairies took the chance to sneak off
in the other direction.

As they crossed the field, the

54

fairies flew a little way away from Katie, so that they could cover more ground. Katie could just make them out, shimmering in the sunlight a few metres away. But soon she was completely absorbed in the search, scanning the ground, the trees and the sky for out-of-place things, and she forgot to check on them.

After about twenty minutes she still hadn't found anything and she began to wonder if they should just plant their marker by the train carriage after all. She waved her arms and called out for them, and the fairies all flew back to her . . . well, all except one.

"Where's Bluebell?" she asked.

The other fairies shrugged.

"We all went in separate directions," Daisy explained. "I'm sure she'll be here in a minute.

Whistle again."

So Katie did, and again, and then she called out, "Bluebell! Bluebell!" as loudly as she could. But still the little fairy didn't appear.

"I can't see her anywhere," said Daisy, her eyes wide with worry.

"Where can she be?" asked Snowdrop nervously.

Even feisty little Rosehip looked frightened.

Katie gazed at the wide, sweeping field. It was huge and Bluebell was tiny. She started to feel very sick.

"Oh, I wish we'd all stayed together," she cried. "I think, maybe, she's lost."

Chapter 5

"Bluebell! Bluebell!"

Bluebell could hear Katie calling in the distance, and she did *try* to answer. But even though she had a very loud voice for a little fairy, her cries of, "I'm here! I'm over here!" were carried away on the wind.

Bluebell knew that if she flew back across the field she could probably spot her friends. But she didn't *want* to fly back. She didn't dare leave her little patch of white

flowers. When she'd spotted them in the distance she'd been curious, so she'd zoomed closer and closer to get a better look.

They were *snowdrops*.

But that was impossible, surely? Excitement thrumming in her chest, she'd zipped right over to them, leaving her fairy friends and Katie far behind in the distance.

"Snowdrops in summer?" she exclaimed. "That doesn't make sense!"

Snowdrops came out at the end of the winter – so it was certainly the wrong *time* for them. And they liked shade and usually grew under trees or at the edges of woodland. In this open field, they were in the wrong *place* too. She touched one and gasped. It was made of silk!

Her heart had started hammering.

"I've found it!" she'd cried. "The real place where the treasure is buried!" She'd done a little dance around the snowdrops to celebrate, stomping her feet and waving her arms in delight. Then she'd taken off into the air, bursting to go and tell the others, and that's when she'd realized – in this vast field there was no way she'd ever find the snowdrops again. She hadn't even been paying attention to which direction she'd flown in, so she didn't even know *roughly* where she was!

"Bluebell! Bluebell!" came the cry again. But this time it sounded even more distant.

Bluebell felt panicky. She wanted to fly back, but she couldn't lose the snowdrops – she was sure they marked the real spot where the

treasure was buried. But then, if she couldn't tell Katie where she was, they couldn't plant the marker.

She pulled a nearby dandelion head off the stalk and blew the white fluff into the air. But of course, Katie didn't notice that. She shouted and waved her arms – with no luck. She hovered in the air directly above the snowdrops and shouted, "Katie! I'm here!" but no one came.

And time was running out.

Bluebell slumped down in a heap beside the snowdrops, feeling thoroughly dejected. What if the treasure hunt ended and they didn't find her in time? What if Katie planted the

marker somewhere else? She wished now that she'd thought it through before going off on her own.

"I've been so silly," she whispered to herself. "I've probably cost us the ruby!"

Suddenly she remembered the strawberry sherbet in her treasure-hunting jacket and decided to have a pinch to cheer herself up, but when she reached into her pocket it wasn't there! Her stitching had come apart and it had all poured away while she was flying! Rosehip was right – her sewing *was* terrible! It was the final straw for Bluebell.

"Oh, everything's gone wrong!" she wailed, and with that she began to sob and sob.

*

At first, when Katie and the fairies realized that Bluebell was lost, they all panicked and rushed off in different directions.

"Come back!" Katie cried. "That's how Bluebell went missing in the first place! Let's go to the four corners of the field and work our way back into the middle. Fly left and right all the way up from your corner, keeping your eyes peeled for Bluebell, OK? If you find her, shout."

"But how will we hear each other?" asked Daisy, frowning with worry. "Our little voices will blow away in the wind."

"You're right," Katie admitted, frowning.

"I've got an idea," said Snowdrop shyly. She dived down and picked

four blades of grass. Then she took a tiny bottle from the pocket of her silky petal skirt and sprinkled a little bit of fairy dust on each one. "I've enchanted the blades of grass so when you blow on them they'll make a really loud whistling sound," she explained.

"That's brilliant, Snowdrop," said Katie, as the little fairy handed them one each.

Katie and the fairies hurried to the four corners of the field and began making careful zigzags back into the middle, searching hard for Bluebell. They looked high in the sky and low on the ground, but none of them could spot her anywhere. The fairies flew slower and slower, their wings drooping and drooping until they almost felt too sad to stay in the air. Katie paced across her own section of the field, her heart pounding with worry, but she couldn't see Bluebell either. It was hopeless!

And that was when Snowdrop spotted something glimmering in the grass and zoomed down for a closer look. It was pink and sparkly, just like . . . she dipped her finger in and licked it. Yes, it was! Wild strawberry sherbet! In a flash she

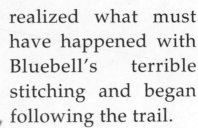

realized what must have happened with Bluebell's terrible stitching and began following the trail.

Just as Katie reached the middle of the field again, Billy's voice came over the tannoy. "Two more minutes, ladies and gents," he announced, "and then that's it. Anyone who hasn't had their guess at where the treasure is yet – you need to get your markers down now." Katie sighed. She still had her marker, but they'd have to forget about the treasure hunt now. Finding Bluebell was far more important.

Daisy and Rosehip came flying back to her, shaking their heads sadly. They hadn't found Bluebell

either. And now Snowdrop had vanished too. What a disaster!

"The treasure hunt will be over soon," said Katie anxiously. "And even if I try to explain about Bluebell, Mum won't believe me. She thinks you fairies are just in my imagination. She'll say we have to go home and. . ." She fell silent, too upset to say more.

The fairies were horrified. They couldn't leave Bluebell and Snowdrop behind, they just couldn't!

Daisy and Rosehip huddled together in a mid-air hug, and Katie could tell that they were both trying their hardest not to cry either.

But just then

there was a high-pitched WHEEEEEEEEEEEEE!!!!!!!!! sound. No one else seemed to even notice it, but Katie and the fairies knew *exactly* what it was.

"Snowdrop's found Bluebell!" they all cried.

Rosehip and Daisy zoomed across the field with Katie sprinting along beneath them.

When they reached the place where the very loud noise had come from, there was Snowdrop, with her arm round Bluebell. Bluebell had red-rimmed eyes and tear-stained cheeks, but she was smiling. And besides her was a patch of snowdrops.

"Quick, put the marker down

here!" she cried.

Katie pulled the marker from her back pocket and planted it, just seconds before Billy declared the treasure hunt officially over.

Suddenly Katie screamed and leaped up as a hand gripping a marker came flying through the air right by her face. Bluebell rolled out of the way under a dock leaf just in time as the marker sliced into the ground exactly where she'd been standing. The patch of snowdrops was now pinned between *two* markers. Katie whirled round.

Tiffany.

"That's not fair! This is *my* place!" Katie shouted. "And anyway, the competition had finished, so you cheated!"

Tiffany just gave her a mean little smile, still puffing and panting from the run.

"I saw you race over here and I knew you were up to something," she said, gasping for air. "I ran and got my marker from beside the railway carriage and followed you here. Even though  you're a boring and weird girl, you're still quite clever, I suppose."

Katie pursed her lips and glared at Tiffany. She had a lot more to say to her, but before she could, Billy called everyone over to him.

Tiffany turned on her heel and marched off. When Katie turned back to the fairies they had swamped Bluebell in a huge hug.

"Oh, we were so worried!" cried Daisy.

"We thought we'd lost you," added Rosehip.

They fluttered up into Katie's arms and she held them all tight. "It's OK. Everything's fine now," she told them.

Bluebell looked up at her with mournful eyes. "But Tiffany . . . she

cheated ... what if she wins the ruby?" she said quietly.

Katie smiled at her. "We've found you and we're back together. That's all that matters," she said gently.

Then, placing the fairies carefully into her bag, she hurried back up to the lane, where everyone was gathering around Billy.

Chapter 6

"Sorry, I didn't have any luck," said Mum, when Katie found her in the crowd.

"It's OK, I found a place," Katie told her. "I just hope I got it right."

They all followed Billy across the field, and when he seemed to be walking away from the railway carriage, there was lots of confused muttering. Katie hardly dared to hope that he would go in the direction of the snowdrops. But

with every step it became clearer that, yes, he was!

Soon they found themselves standing beside the little clump of white flowers. As some of the people saw them there were whispers of "Oh!" and "I see!" but others still looked confused.

Katie grinned up at Mum. "That's my marker," she told her proudly.

The surprise on Mum's face was a picture!

"It was a difficult clue," said Billy, "but two of you seem to have worked it out."

Katie and Tiffany stepped forward and Billy told everyone about the pretend snowdrops.

Katie's heart was thudding. If she and the fairies were just a smidgen out, then Tiffany would win the ruby. It was so awful that she could

hardly bear to think about it.

Katie held her breath as Billy took a long stick from his pocket and pushed it into the soil right beside Tiffany's marker. The whole stick went down into the ground. Katie wasn't sure what that meant, but she crossed her fingers for luck as Billy pulled up the stick and pushed it into the ground beside her own marker. It stopped halfway and wouldn't go any further. She blinked at it. Was that good or bad? She didn't know!

Then he turned and smiled at her. "Ladies and gentlemen," he said, "I think we have a winner. Let's find out!"

He handed Katie a little trowel and motioned for her to dig down into the soil. As she did, the trowel struck something solid and she levered it up

and pulled it out. It was a tiny treasure chest. She opened it slowly, her hands shaking, hardly daring to look. But yes – there was the ruby!

Everyone clapped and cheered, and Mum was beside herself with happiness. Only Tiffany didn't join in, but instead pulled a face like she was sucking a lemon. The fairies zoomed out of Katie's bag and tumbled about in the air, twirling and diving and turning loop-the-loops of joy. In fact, they were celebrating so much they almost gave themselves away: several children looked up and

blinked, thinking they had spotted something strange in the sunlight!

Tiffany scowled at Katie. "That ruby's half mine!" she mumbled, staring at the treasure chest with greedy eyes.

"No, it's not," said Katie. "*You* were the one who didn't want to work together, remember? *You* insisted on finders keepers and *you* made Billy give you your own marker. So I think it's definitely ours – I mean *mine.*"

"That's not fair!" whined Tiffany. The fairies giggled overhead as she stomped back to the car.

"I do apologize," Mum said again, weakly, to the lady beside her. "She's not my daughter."

But not even one of Tiffany's most revolting strops could spoil the magical moment for Katie and the

fairies. They'd actually done it! They'd won the ruby!

Katie placed the little treasure chest carefully into her bag and then gave Mum a big hug.

"Well done, darling," said Mum.

"Thanks," said Katie, "but I couldn't have done it without my fairy friends!"

Mum laughed and squeezed Katie even tighter. "You've still got those imaginary friends, have you?" she cried. "How lovely!"

"Yes, they certainly are," said Katie, winking at them as they zoomed back into her bag for the journey home.

Of course, Tiffany had sulked in the car and hadn't even said thank you to Mum when she'd dropped her home. But Mum and Katie didn't

mind; they were just relieved that she'd gone!

Ten minutes later, the ruby was safely locked away in Katie's jewellery box, along with the other birthstones that they had collected. Mum had suggested making the ruby into a necklace, but Katie had just smiled a secret smile to herself and said she liked it best exactly as it was. Then she'd kissed Mum goodbye and skipped out into the garden, and soon she was back down at the Fairy House with her four friends.

Rosehip played fairy songs on the piano while they all had a big celebration singsong, complete with dancing, skipping, spinning, twirling and jumping for joy.

After five of their favourite fairy songs, they fell into a giggling heap

on the living-room rug, and Rosehip squished on too.

"Snowdrop, I just have to know one thing," said Katie. "How *did* you find Bluebell in that huge field?"

Snowdrop giggled and explained about the trail of wild strawberry sherbet.

"See, Bluebell, I told you your

sewing was awful!" said Rosehip.

"Actually, I planned for that pocket to have a hole in all along," Bluebell retorted. "The stitching was like that on purpose, so that the sherbet would fall out. It was especially designed as an anti-getting-lost pocket – and it worked, so there!"

Rosehip raised her eyebrows and Daisy stifled a giggle.

"*Of course* it was, Bluebell," said Katie, hiding a grin. "Only six more birthstones to collect now!" she added cheerily. "Soon we'll have them all and we'll be able to work the magic to save the tree!"

"Hooray!" cried the fairies.

Katie jumped up and said, "How about a game of fairy skipping?"

"Now *that*," said Bluebell, "is a very good idea."

And with that they all sprang to their feet, grabbed each other's hands and hurried out into the late-afternoon sunshine.

The End

Bluebell
Spring fairy

Likes:

blue, blue, blue and more blue,
turning somersaults in the air, dancing

Dislikes:

coming second, being told what to do

Daisy
Summer fairy

Likes:

everyone to be friends, bright sunshine,
cheery yellow colours, smiling

Dislikes:

arguments, cold dark places,
orange nylon dresses

Rosehip
Autumn fairy

Likes:

riding magic ponies, telling Bluebell
what to do, playing the piano, singing

Dislikes:

keeping quiet, boring colours,
not being the centre of attention!

Snowdrop
Winter fairy

Likes:

singing fairy songs, cool quiet places, riding her
favourite magical unicorn, making snowfairies

Dislikes:

being too hot, keeping secrets

Don't miss the rest of the series!

The Fairy House

Fairy Friends

Snowdrop x

Kelly McKain